ANDREW WANTS A DOG

STEVEN KROLL

ILLUSTRATIONS BY
MOLLY DELANEY

HYPERION BOOKS
FOR
CHILDREN

For information address
Hyperion Books for Children,
114 Fifth Avenue, New York, New York 10011.
FIRST EDITION
1   3   5   7   9   10   8   6   4   2

Library of Congress Cataloging-in-Publication Data
Kroll, Steven.
    Andrew wants a dog/by Steven Kroll; illustrations by
Molly Delaney—1st ed.
        p.   cm.
    Summary: When his father refuses to let him have a dog,
seven-year-old Andrew decides to become one, with the help
of a very realistic dog costume from a magic shop.
    ISBN 1-56282-118-0—ISBN 1-56282-119-9 (lib. bdg.)
    [1. Dogs—Fiction. 2. Costume—Fiction.] I. Delaney,
Molly, ill. II. Title.
PZ7.K9225Amr 1992
[E]—dc20   91-25637
                                                          CIP
                                                          AC

For
Kendall and Phyllis Merriam

CONTENTS

1. WANTING   1
2. DUKE   11
3. MR. MAGIC   23
4. DOGS WILL BE DOGS   31
5. COFFEE SHOP SURPRISE   39
6. EVERYONE LOVES A COSTUME   47

1 WANTING

Andrew had a room full of games and toys. He had a big stuffed bear, a big stuffed giraffe, a big stuffed tiger, a computer, and a bicycle. He was a very fast runner and even had some medals for winning races. He did well in school and had a best friend named Bernie.

There was just one thing Andrew didn't have. He didn't have a dog.

Ever since he'd first walked past the pet shop on Oak Street, Andrew had wanted a real live dog. There were little cocker spaniel puppies in the window that first time. They were tumbling and running around in the torn newspaper, yipping and nipping at each other's heels.

He'd been very little then, only about three or four, and all he wanted to do was pick up one of those puppies and hold it in his arms. He squeezed his mother's hand extra tight. "Mom," he said, "could I please have a dog?"

"Oh, Andrew," said his mom, "you're too little to have a dog. Maybe when you're older."

Older, thought Andrew. How much older is older?

He was almost eight now, well, really only seven and a half, and every time he walked past the Oak Street pet shop, he still wanted a dog. Sometimes there were beagle puppies in the window. He wanted one. Sometimes there were basset hound puppies. He wanted one of those. Sometimes there were Irish setters. He wanted one of those, too.

The Irish setter puppies were especially cute. They were all red and fuzzy looking, and they kept tripping over their paws, which were too big for them. When Andrew got home, he marched up to his mom and said, for the umpteenth time, "Mom, I'm older now. Could I have a dog?"

And for the umpteenth time, Mom replied, "I wouldn't mind, Andrew, but I'm not sure about your father. You'll have to ask him, too."

All through dinner, Andrew was very nervous. He poked at his piece of chicken. He pushed the peas around on his plate. He barely touched his glass of milk.

When dessert came, it was chocolate pudding, Andrew's favorite. He pushed it away. He couldn't even look at it.

"Andrew," said his father, "why aren't you eating?"

"I'm not hungry," said Andrew.

"But you're usually such a good eater, Andrew. What's the matter?"

Andrew bit his lip. He summoned up all his courage. "Dad," he said, "could I have a dog?"

There was a silence. Dad put down his spoon and tried not to frown. "I don't think so, Andrew. Dogs are too hard to take care of."

"But I'd take care of him," Andrew said. "I'd feed him and pet him and take him for walks."

"He's very good with animals, Wesley," said Mom. "I'm sure he'd do a good job with a dog."

Dad looked sadly from Andrew to Mom. "You know I don't like dogs, Margaret. They fall all over you and make a terrible mess."

"I'd clean up the mess," said Andrew. "He'd stay with me, and I'd take him to the vet if he got sick."

Dad smiled a little. "I'm glad to hear that, Andrew, but don't you think you'd get tired of this dog? You'd go off to play with your friends, and your mom and I would end up looking after him."

"I wouldn't get tired," said Andrew. "He'd be my friend."

"Well," said Dad, "the real problem is I just don't like dogs, but I will agree to think about it."

Back in his room, Andrew sat on the bed. He put his elbows on his knees and his chin in his hands. He thought about how wonderful it would be to have a dog.

He would teach it to heel and to fetch and to catch a rubber ball in its mouth. He would let it jump in his lap and lick his face. He would get all dressed up in his raincoat, rainhat, and rubbers and take it for a walk under a special big umbrella, no matter how hard it rained. He would housebreak it so well there would be no messes anywhere, and if the dog got sick, he would carry it to the vet in his arms. Mom would have to drive, but that wouldn't be too much to ask, would it?

Andrew smiled. Every night, when he got into bed, the dog would curl up right beside him and keep him warm.

But what would it take to convince his father, who didn't like dogs? Andrew had no idea.

The next day, when he got home from

school, his mom said, "Want to come visit Mrs. Gunther? She invited me over for tea."

Mrs. Gunther was the old lady who lived next door. She was little and stooped and had a bristly chin. She always tried to kiss Andrew and he had to duck away, but he really quite liked her anyway.

"Sure, I'll come," he said. "Just give me a minute to wash up."

A minute after that they were climbing the steps to Mrs. Gunther's house. When she opened the door, a big black cocker spaniel came leaping out at them.

It ran around, barking and sniffing. It jumped up on Andrew and licked his hand. When he bent to pet it, the dog licked his face. It looked just like an older version of the puppies he had seen when he was little.

"My goodness," said Andrew's mother, "where did you get that dog?"

"Mouser was my son's dog," said Mrs. Gunther. "The family thought I should have company, so my son gave him to me."

"But isn't Mouser a cat's name?"

"My son has some strange ideas about things."

But there was nothing strange about the dog. All through the serving of tea in the living room, Mouser lay curled up in Andrew's lap. It was so impossible to move him that Andrew couldn't reach the cookies on the table. Finally, Mrs. Gunther had to stick the plate right under Andrew's nose.

"That dog really likes you," Mrs. Gunther said.

Andrew smiled. "I like him, too."

When it was time to leave, the dog followed Andrew to the door. As they thanked Mrs. Gunther and reached the front steps, she said, "You don't happen to have any mice, do you?"

"Certainly not," said Andrew's mother. "Why do you ask?"

"We could test out Mouser's name."

"Oh, Mom," said Andrew, "we must have one or two."

Andrew's mom gave him a very serious look. When they got home, she said, "How could you even suggest to Mrs. Gunther that we had mice?"

"I'm sorry," said Andrew. "I thought that way we could try having a dog for a while. He was such a great dog, too."

"Andrew," said his mother, "that dog is Mrs. Gunther's dog. Now, I know how much you want one and you know I wouldn't mind, but you heard what your father said. He's thinking about it."

And that was the end of that.

2 DUKE

The following Sunday, Andrew went to spend the afternoon at his best friend Bernie's house. As Andrew climbed the steps, Bernie's mom flung open the door. "Hurry!" she said. "Bernie's in his room. He's got a surprise."

Andrew dashed into the house. What could the surprise be? He hoped it would be something for him.

He hurried down the hall. As he approached Bernie's room, he heard giggles from behind the door. He turned the knob, and there was Bernie, lying in the middle of the floor with a fuzzy brown-and-black German shepherd puppy.

"Hi," Bernie said. "Look what I've got."

Andrew was speechless. Was this Bernie's puppy? Or had Bernie been given the puppy as a surprise for *him*? "What is this?" he finally blurted.

"This is a German shepherd puppy, silly," said Bernie. "Mom and Dad gave him to me this morning. He's an early birthday present."

Andrew's hopes collapsed. "Oh," he said, and tried not to cry.

"What's the matter with you?" said Bernie. "Come in and play with Duke. He's going to be really big someday."

Andrew sank to his knees, and the puppy waddled over to him, its little tail wagging. Andrew patted the furry head, and the puppy licked his hand.

"Let's play!" Bernie shouted. He tackled the puppy and scooped it up in his arms. The puppy yipped and playfully tried to bite his nose. He put the puppy down, and it chased him and Andrew around the room.

Then Andrew lay down on the floor, and the puppy jumped on him and licked his face. Andrew turned over, and the puppy squealed and scrambled onto unsteady feet. It got so overexcited, it peed a little on the floor.

"Uh-oh," said Bernie, and he ran and got some paper towels.

Nobody seemed to mind about the accident, and Bernie and Andrew went on playing with Duke until it was time for a snack of cookies and milk. After that, Andrew had to go home.

"See you in school tomorrow," Bernie shouted after him.

"Yeah, see you," said Andrew, but all he could think about was puppies.

In the car going home, his mom asked, "Did you have a good time? How is Bernie?"

"Bernie's fine," said Andrew. "His parents gave him a German shepherd puppy. The puppy's name is Duke."

"Oh," said Andrew's mom.

There was a silence. Then Andrew said, "Mom, could I *please* have a dog? Please, please, please!"

Mom pulled over to the side of the road. "Andrew," she said, "I understand exactly how you feel, but you know my answer.

Your father has to agree."

That night, dinner was the worst ever. Andrew was so nervous he could hardly look at his food, no less eat it. When dessert came and went without his touching it, his father said, "Is this about the dog, Andrew?"

Andrew nodded weakly.

"His friend Bernie was given a puppy this morning," Mom said.

"I see," Dad said.

Andrew wondered if Bernie's puppy would make the difference. He hoped against hope.

"I've been doing a lot of thinking," Dad said. "I know how much you want this dog—"

Please, thought Andrew, please say yes.

"—but I just don't believe you're ready. A boy has to be a little older before he takes on such responsibility. I don't want to be critical of Bernie's parents, but when you're twelve or thirteen—"

There it was again. Older, always older. Now he would have to be twelve or thirteen. When he was twelve or thirteen, he would have to be sixteen or seventeen. His father wouldn't like dogs then either. Andrew got up from the table and ran to his room.

He threw himself on the bed and covered his head with a pillow. He would never get to take his very own dog for a

walk. He would never teach him to heel and fetch and catch a rubber ball in his mouth. It was just no use.

He fell asleep in his clothes and had to take them off when he woke up in the middle of the night. Then he fell asleep again, and when he woke up in the morning, he was feeling better.

Since he hadn't eaten any dinner, he was also very hungry. He got dressed, trooped downstairs to the kitchen, and there were his parents, already having breakfast.

"Hi, Andrew," said Mom.

"Morning, Andrew," said Dad.

"Hi," said Andrew, and sat down to two full bowls of Cheerios with bananas and a huge glass of milk. No one said a thing about last night. It was probably just as well.

Andrew sighed and picked up his schoolbag. He kissed his parents goodbye and began his walk to school.

When he reached the corner, there was

a fat woman walking a Pekingese. She had long, skinny legs and a big round hat that seemed too big for her. The dog was bouncing along on its little legs, puffing and snorting and sniffing the ground. Every so often, the fat woman would stoop down with great difficulty and pat the dog on its head.

Andrew tried not to be depressed by the good time they were obviously having. He remembered he was supposed to be feeling better, took a deep breath, and walked on. But then he saw a little old man patting a collie tied to a parking meter and a brown-and-white fox terrier staring out the hardware store window. He saw a boxer jogging with a woman in a sweatsuit and a dachshund waiting in a car and a great big sheepdog sitting on someone's front steps.

Everyone seemed to have a dog except him! By the time he got to school, Andrew was a wreck.

He sank into his seat and looked at the

floor. "Hello, Andrew," said his teacher, Mrs. Henderson, but all Andrew could do was nod vaguely in her direction.

He couldn't concentrate on math. Language arts was a blur. Gym was no fun, just a lot of boring exercises. As he finished up his jumping jacks, Andrew noticed how much Mr. Martin, the gym teacher, looked like a bulldog. Katie, the girl next to him, looked exactly like a French poodle.

/ 19 /

Then came lunch. Bernie sat down with Andrew as usual. "How did you like Duke?" he asked. "Isn't he the cutest thing you ever saw?"

Andrew nodded.

"He slept right next to me in bed last night, and he ate all his food this morning."

Andrew nodded again.

"Do you think your parents will ever let you have a dog?"

Andrew shook his head and turned away.

"Do you want to eat by yourself?"

Andrew looked up at Bernie sadly. Bernie took his tray and moved across the cafeteria.

3 MR. MAGIC

When school was out, Andrew walked home alone. Everything seemed dark and gloomy. He would never have a dog. He would never even look at dogs anymore. He would just be lonely and miserable forever.

On Main Street, he stopped to look in the window of a shop called Mr. Magic. It was a weird sort of place, full of rubberized skull masks, Dracula capes, oddly marked cards, and big false teeth, but Andrew loved it. In fact, it was his favorite shop, and he frequently stopped in to see the owner, who called himself Mr. Magic, just to say hello.

As he peered in the window, Andrew noticed something he had never seen before. It was a dog suit that looked exactly like a golden retriever. There was a zipper down the middle that would make climbing in and out easy.

Andrew stared at the dog suit for a long time. Even though he knew he would never have a dog, he couldn't help wanting one. If he couldn't have a dog but still

YES, WE'RE OPEN!

wanted one, maybe he could be one in-stead! It wouldn't be quite the same thing, but pretending to be a dog would make him feel better about not having one. All he had to do was put on this dog suit. . . .

Andrew smiled and walked into the shop. There was a pile of rubber chickens in a corner and rows of wolf, dog, frog, monkey, clown, and Frankenstein masks along the walls. Mr. Magic was standing at the counter.

"Hi, Andrew," said Mr. Magic, "how are you today?"

"I'd like to try on the dog suit," Andrew said.

Mr. Magic grinned, revealing two neat rows of very small teeth. "Why, sure," he said. "You know, I just got that suit in today. You're the very first person to try it on."

Andrew grinned to himself. No one in town knew about this suit. No one would ever suspect he was inside it. Just think of the fun he could have!

Mr. Magic brought out the suit, and

Andrew stepped into it. A pretty comfort-
able fit, and the moment he had it on, he
loved it. He could sort of wag the tail by
moving his bottom, and the jaws opened
and closed when he opened and closed
his mouth.

He marched up to the counter and
poked his head through the zipper in the
middle. "I'd like to wear this home," he

said. "Would it be okay if I paid you my two dollars allowance now and the rest as soon as I have it?"

Mr. Magic grinned again. "Sure, Andrew. I know I can trust you."

Andrew tried walking around the shop to get in practice. It was difficult walking on all fours like a dog, even more difficult trying to imitate the lope of a golden retriever. The legs of the costume were a little tight around his arms and legs, and when he tried to stretch them out and pick up speed, they would pull and somehow get crossed over one another. He had to concentrate very hard and make sure he was moving his right arm and right leg forward and his left arm and left leg back, but the more he concentrated, the better he got and the shape of the costume seemed to make the whole thing more natural. He began to feel more and more like a dog. He looked in the mirror, and he *looked* like a dog. In less than half an hour, he was ready.

He left the shop, poking the door open with his nose. He started down Main Street, and there was Bernie, waiting for the light to change.

Andrew the Dog squatted on his haunches next to Bernie. Bernie looked down. "Wow!" he said, "a dog." He patted Andrew on the head. "Nice doggie," he said, "nice doggie."

Andrew the Dog stuck out his tongue and licked Bernie's face.

Bernie laughed and tried to protect himself. "You're almost as cute as my Duke," he said as Andrew went on licking him. A moment later, the light changed.

"Uh-oh, gotta go," said Bernie. "Nice meeting you, dog."

Panting a little, Andrew watched Bernie dash across the street. His tongue was dry and sore from so much licking, but he didn't care. He tried to imagine Bernie's face if he ever told him who had been licking it. It didn't matter. He was a dog now.

4 DOGS WILL BE DOGS

Andrew picked himself up on all fours. He checked out the legs and paws of the costume and waggled his tail. Then he loped across Main Street into Montrose Park.

It was getting to be late in the afternoon, and there weren't too many people around. He saw a man on a bench and a couple walking hand in hand. Then he saw a very little girl toddling around in front of a stroller. A skinny woman in a dark coat was sitting nearby. She had to be the little girl's mom.

Did the little girl like dogs? Andrew padded over and sniffed her.

The little girl stopped, looked at him, and wobbled a little on her feet. Then she began pounding him on the nose. "Dog-gie!" she yelled. "Dog-gie!"

Uh-oh, thought Andrew. This is not so great.

The girl's mom was on her feet. "That's enough, Melanie. You leave that dog alone!" she said with her hands on her hips.

It seemed a good time to make tracks, and Andrew did exactly that. He loped on through the park, discovering more and more how easy it was to keep his four legs moving together. Then he stopped and tried a little bark.

"Ruff!" he said. "Ruff, ruff!"

He looked around, but no one seemed to have heard. A moment later, he came upon two boys playing catch in a field.

They were playing with a rubber ball, and Andrew watched them throw it back and forth. Then one boy threw the ball very high and far, so high and far it went clear over the other boy's head. Well, why not? thought Andrew. He raced after the ball, picked it up in his mouth, and returned it to the boy who had done the throwing.

"Good dog," said the boy, patting Andrew on the head. "Here—fetch!"

He threw the ball a very long way, and Andrew romped after it. He was really enjoying himself, but this time he was concentrating so hard on the ball that he lost his footing, got his paws crossed over one another, and fell down. Uh-oh, he thought, I've really done it now. He picked himself up, got the ball wedged between his dog teeth, and returned it nervously to the first boy.

"You poor old clumsy thing," the first boy said, patting Andrew on the head and rubbing his tummy. "You're really not so good at this, are you?"

Instantly, Andrew was all dog again. He lay down on his back, put his legs in the air, and let his tummy be stroked.

The zipper down the middle was completely covered in fur, and the boy was so eager to be friendly he would never have begun to notice. He stroked and patted until, finally, he said to his friend, "Hey, Roger, why don't you have him fetch?"

He tossed the ball to Roger, who threw it low but far. Andrew romped after it, and the game began again. After a while, though, he got bored. When the boys decided to rest and the moment seemed right, he looked across the field as if he'd seen his master, gave a few practiced ruffs, and ran away.

"Bye, dog!" shouted Roger.

"Bye, dog!" shouted Roger's friend.

All that running and fetching had tired Andrew out. He flopped down behind a bush to rest. He was back on his feet and sort of trotting down a path when suddenly a huge Great Dane appeared. The Dane was attached to a leash, but the large man at the other end was getting pulled in all directions.

"Stop, Bertrand!" the man shouted, but Bertrand paid no attention, pulled the man off his feet, swooped down upon the helpless Andrew, and began sniffing him everywhere.

For a moment Andrew found this amusing, but when Bertrand wouldn't stop and got even more determined, Andrew began backing away.

Bertrand didn't like that at all. His legs stiffened, and his mouth twisted into a snarl. He bared his huge, sharp teeth and began to growl. Then he began to bark.

Uh-oh, thought Andrew, it's time to get out of here. A few ruffs would clearly be of no use, and he took off down the path just as Bertrand reared back, lunged forward, and snapped at his tail!

Fortunately, Bertrand's master had regained his feet by this time, and even though he promptly lost them again and fell on his face, he managed to keep a firm hold on the leash. The leather

snapped taut, but Bertrand wasn't going anywhere.

But Andrew was. He headed for the exit as fast as his four legs could carry him. All the way there, he heard Bertrand barking and growling, and as he reached the street, he heard the large man say, "Well, dogs will be dogs."

Well, not this dog, thought Andrew. It was definitely time for a little rest and re-laxation.

5 COFFEE SHOP SURPRISE

Andrew sat and waited for the light to change so he could cross back onto Main Street. As the signal flashed green, he saw a short blond woman, a friend of his mother's called Mrs. Clark, open the door to the coffee shop on the corner. Andrew dashed across the road and scooted in under her arm.

The coffee shop felt warm and cozy, the perfect place to catch his breath. As he padded in behind Mrs. Clark, she noticed him. "Look at this sweet dog," she said. She stooped to pat his head. "He must be hungry, John. Give him something to eat."

John Duffy, the coffee shop owner, leaned over the counter. "Good dog," he said. "Have a cookie."

The big chocolate chip cookie looked extra delicious in John Duffy's hand. Andrew reached up and took it in his dog mouth. Suddenly he was very hungry. Oh, how he wanted this cookie, but it was tricky sliding it through the dog teeth to his own. Carefully he got his own teeth around the edge, but as he took a bite, a piece slipped down into the costume and the rest fell on the floor.

Andrew dropped his head, but before he could rescue the larger piece, he heard John Duffy say, "Better call the dogcatcher. This pooch has no collar. Who knows where he came from."

Uh-oh, thought Andrew. He forgot about the cookie and leaped for the door.

"Stop that dog!" he heard, but fortunately the door opened outward and he was now speedy enough on four legs to be able to push it open and run off before anyone could catch him.

But where could he go? John Duffy, Mrs. Clark, anyone who wanted to would be after him. Not to mention the dogcatcher.

He turned the corner and loped down a block of houses with long flights of stairs leading up to their front porches. At the top of one long flight was a newspaper.

If I pick up that newspaper and deliver it to the owner of the house, perhaps he will take me inside, thought Andrew. He will be grateful. He will pet me and protect me.

Andrew bounded up the stairs. As he took the newspaper in his mouth, the door flew open. A tall, thin woman with frizzy red hair rushed out at him with a rolling pin.

"Thief!" she shouted, swinging the pin. "Drop that newspaper. Help! Thief!"

Andrew dropped the paper. He fled down the stairs just as John Duffy, Mrs. Clark, and two waitresses from the coffee shop rounded the corner.

Uh-oh, thought Andrew, and took off down the block. John Duffy, Mrs. Clark, and the two waitresses from the coffee shop shouted after him. "Help! Thief!" yelled the red-haired woman once again, though the newspaper in question was still back on her front porch. She, too, joined the group chasing Andrew.

It was a good thing he was such a fast runner, but Andrew himself was starting to get tired of this game. He loved being a successful dog, but it wasn't so terrific to be dressed up in a dog suit and get chased by half your hometown. He was feeling pretty sweaty inside the costume, the legs were tight and scratchy, and the missing piece of cookie had somehow found its way into his left front paw, where it made running like a dog that much more difficult and painful besides.

He turned a corner and was about ready to tear off the costume when he heard, "Here, doggie, here, doggie."

He looked, and there was a smiling little boy. The boy was standing in an alley, and Andrew, now very exhausted, thought he must be trying to show him a way to escape.

"Here, doggie, here, doggie," the boy said again, and Andrew trotted over.

"Look what I have for you!" said the boy. He pulled out a big, disgusting bone and thrust it into Andrew's face.

The bone smelled horrible. Bits of rotten meat clung to the end. "Oh, yuk!" Andrew said out loud.

The boy paid no attention to the fact that this dog had just talked. He jumped on Andrew's back and began kicking him in the ribs.

"Ride 'em, cowboy!" he shouted.

Enough was enough. Andrew stood up and let the boy drop to the ground. Then he ran off down the block on two legs, a boy in a dog suit pursued by John Duffy, Mrs. Clark, two waitresses from the coffee shop, a red-haired woman with a rolling pin, and a frowning little boy waving a disgusting bone.

Now was the time to get that dog suit off. As he ran, Andrew tried to unzip the zipper, but the zipper wouldn't budge. He tried again. Nothing.

Uh-oh, he thought. What am I going to do now?

6 EVERYONE LOVES A COSTUME

Andrew ran down another block and doubled back onto Main Street. As he passed by Mr. Magic's shop, Mr. Magic himself appeared at the door.

With great relief, Andrew stumbled into the shop.

"Oh, thank you," he said, and slumped to the floor. "Mr. Magic," he said, "could you please help me with this zipper?"

Mr. Magic smiled down at him, revealing once again those two neat rows of very small teeth. He paid absolutely no attention to Andrew's question.

"You've been so successful with this

costume," he said instead, "and it is very appropriate that you have come by at this time. The shop is closed, and I'm giving a party for my most satisfied customers. I would like you to join us."

"You would?" said Andrew.

"Yes," said Mr. Magic. "Come with me. The party is in the back room."

Andrew was very nervous. He hadn't counted on a party. All he really wanted was to get the dog suit off, but Mr. Magic was already escorting him to the back room.

The room was as bright as day. All the lights were on, and in the middle of a long table was a huge cake bursting with lit candles. There were streamers and balloons, and around the table there were people dressed in costumes.

There was a horse, a cow, and a frog. There was a monkey, a goat, a lion, a clown, and a duck.

"Isn't this wonderful?" Mr. Magic was saying. "Everyone looks so perfect. Everyone loves a costume."

"Mr. Magic," said Andrew, "Mr. Magic, could you please help me with this zipper?"

"Andrew," said Mr. Magic, "you must have a piece of cake. It's all chocolate, and I baked it myself. Here, let me give you some."

Andrew didn't want any cake. He didn't want to be at this party. He wanted to be home and out of this dog suit.

"No, thank you," he said, and broke away from Mr. Magic. He ran through the shop and out the door, looked right and left for the dogcatcher, ran and ran, took a shortcut through the park, and ran toward home.

But he ran out of breath before he got there. He sank down under a tree to rest.

At that moment, a very large alley cat appeared. It arched its back. It crept closer, hissing and baring its teeth.

"Uh-oh," said Andrew, too tired to fight or flee. "You don't like dogs, and you're after me, too!"

He couldn't pull off the costume, but he had to do something. Summoning all his strength, he jumped up and began climbing the tree. It was a tough climb, but somehow he reached the top. Unfortunately, the mean old cat climbed right up after him!

Andrew was cornered. The only thing he could do now was climb out to the end of a branch and hope he could jump to the ground without hurting himself. He jumped, landed, and looked up. The cat

was cowering at the end of the branch,
too chicken to jump!

"Whoopee!" shouted Andrew, and ran
the rest of the way home. He was so exhausted when he got there he sprawled
headlong on his doorstep.

A moment later, the door opened and
his mother peeked out. "Oh no, this poor
dog!" she said. "Wesley, help me."

Together his parents picked him up and
carried him into the kitchen. Gently, they
placed him on the floor. His mom got a
pillow and put it under his head. His dad
covered him with a blanket.

"Let's see what he might like to eat," Mom said, pulling out some leftover hamburger from the fridge.

"I'll get a dish of water," said Dad.

"Mom, Dad," said Andrew, "it's me."

"What?" said Mom.

"What?" said Dad.

They whirled around.

"It's me, Andrew."

He gave the zipper on his dog suit a yank. There wasn't an ounce of dogginess left in him, and this time the zipper worked. He stepped out of the costume and smiled at his parents.

They looked at him in amazement.

"Oh, Andrew, that costume, your voice, I've never been so scared!" Mom said. She hugged him. So did his dad.

Andrew hugged them back. He smiled. "I guess you both like dogs more than you thought."

"You know, I think you're right," said Dad, laughing. "Let's go talk in the living room."

When they were all sitting down, with Dad in his wing chair and Mom and Andrew on the couch, Dad seemed to be fumbling for the right words.

"I'm sorry I was so late," Andrew said finally, hopefully.

"We're just glad you're home," Mom said.

Still nothing from Dad, so Andrew explained about the costume and what had happened. He left out the part about how he'd sort of really felt like a dog for a while.

Dad leaned forward in his chair. "That is really something. You're just a boy, and you did all that." He paused. "Son, there's a lot I've had to change my mind about today, but at the top of the list—"

"Oh, good!" said Mom.

"Oh, Dad!" said Andrew.

"Shall we go to the pet shop tomorrow?" Dad asked.

"Yes," said Mom.

"Oh, yes!" said Andrew.

The dream was coming true. It really was.